World of Readi

Disney Junior

MARVEL

Spidey and his Amazing Friends

House-Sitting at Tony's

Adapted by **Steve Behling**
Based on the episode written by **Ken Kristensen**
Illustrated by **Premise Entertainment**

MARVEL
Los Angeles • New York

Team Spidey visits
Tony Stark's home.
Tony is Iron Man!

"Come inside!" says Tony.

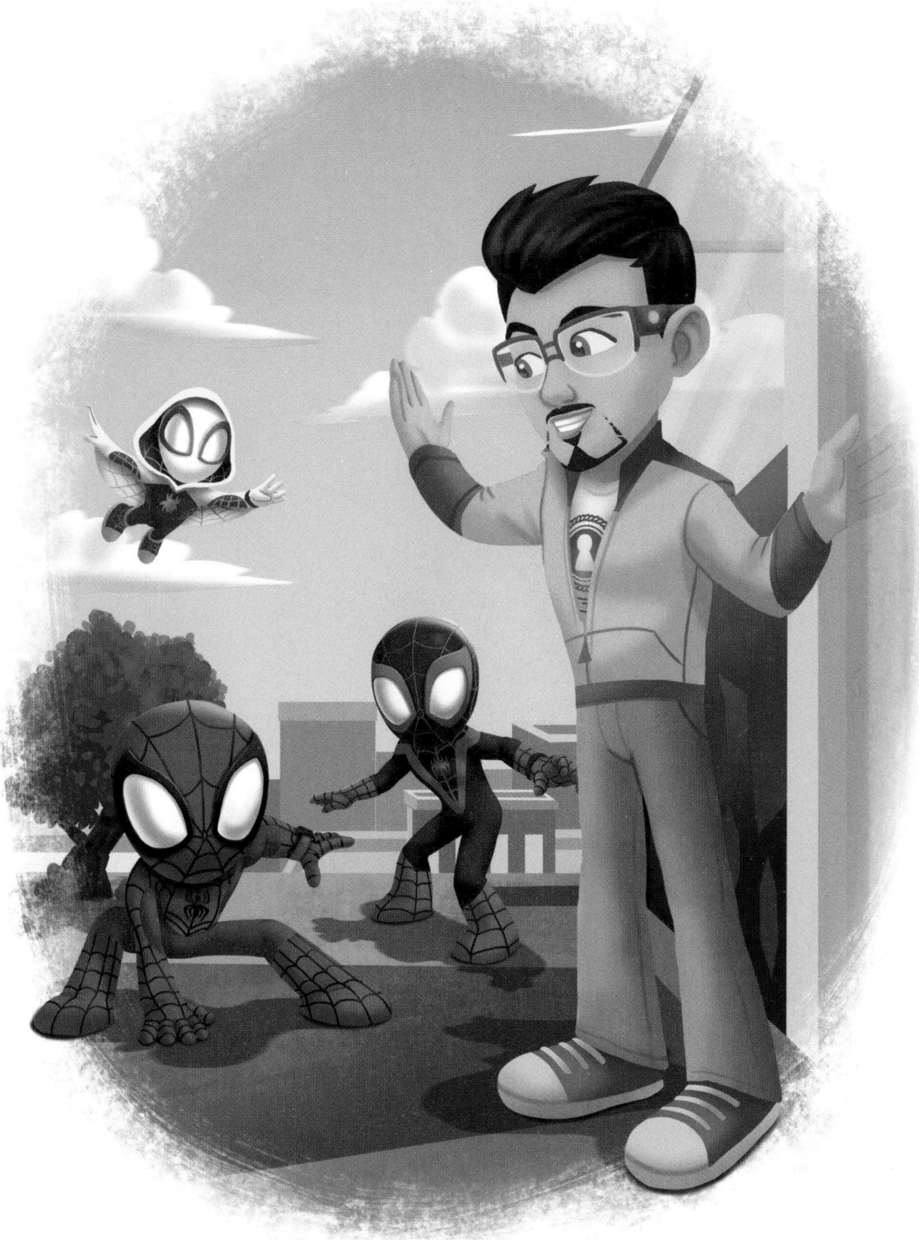

Just then, Peter trips
on a pool toy.

Tony shows his home
to Team Spidey.

"This is a Boom Ball,"
Tony says.
"It plays music!"

The heroes go to
Tony's workshop.

Oh, no. It's Electro!

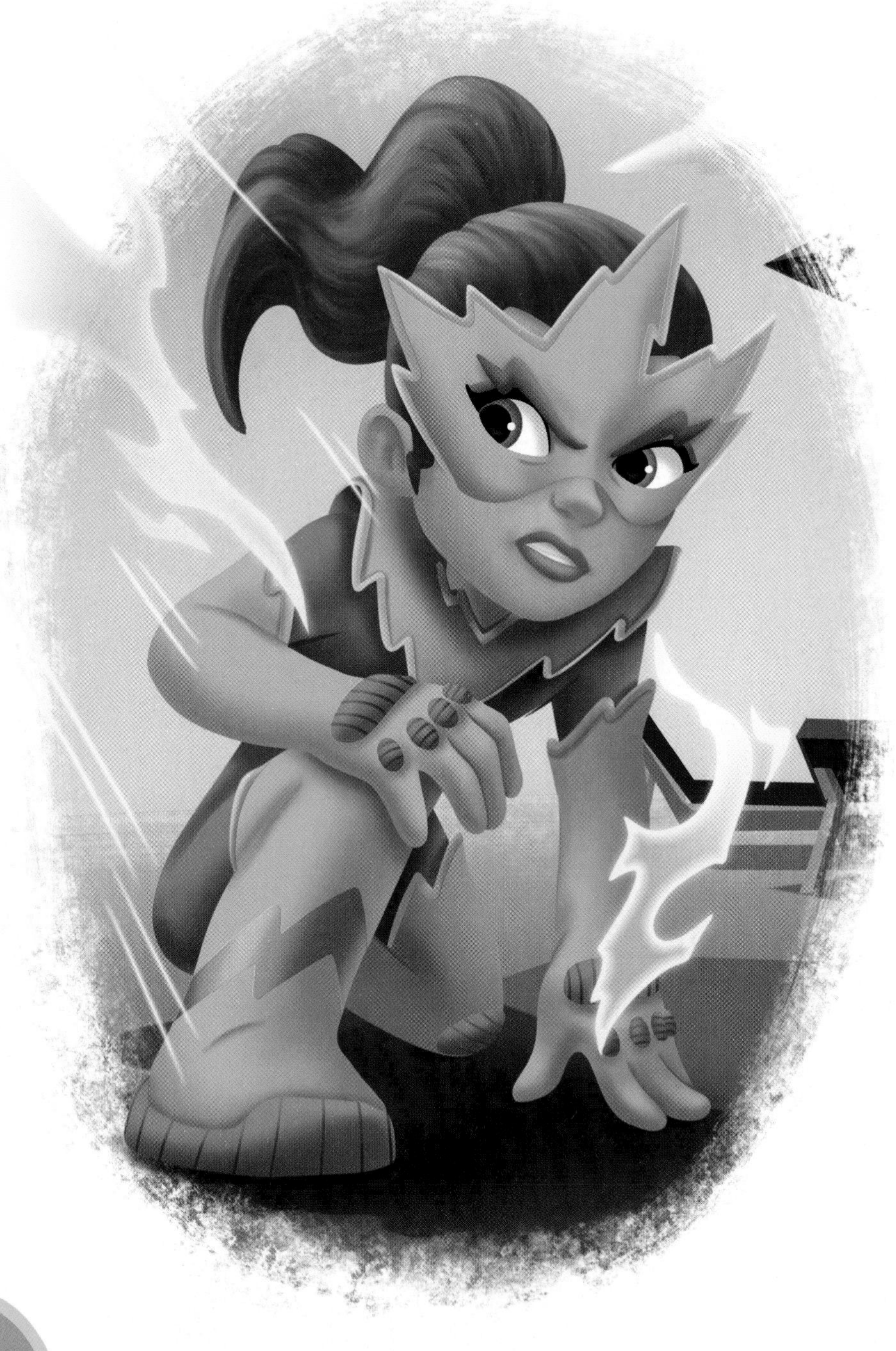

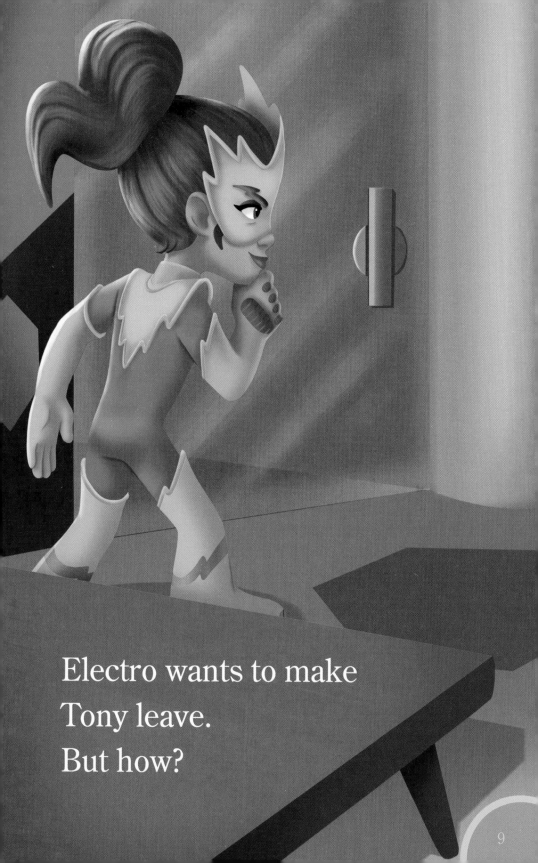

Electro wants to make
Tony leave.
But how?

Tony shows off his
Iron Man suits.

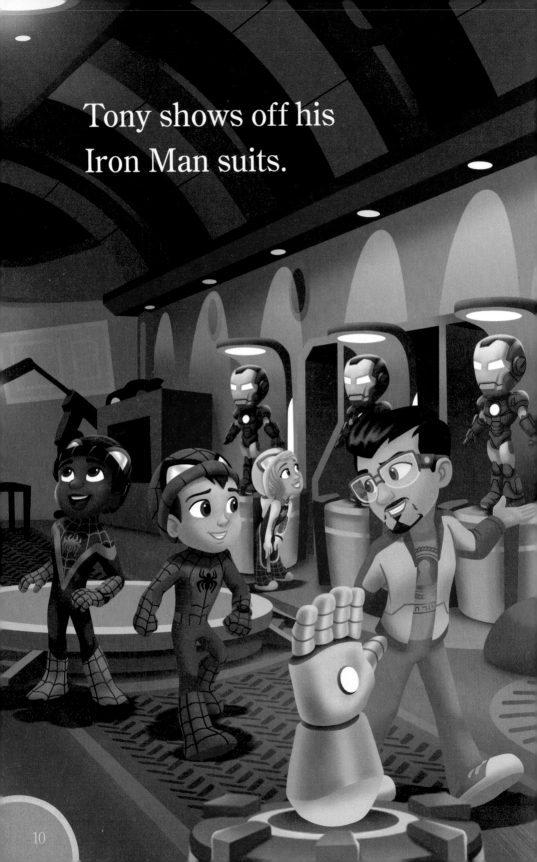

"I made these gloves,"
Tony says.
"Each one has a power."

Peter tries the blue glove.
It sprays water!

Tony's phone rings.
"The mayor wants to
see you," the caller says.

But it's just Electro
playing a prank!

Tony puts on his Iron Man suit.
He leaves.

"Bye-bye, Iron Man!"
Electro says.
She goes inside Tony's house.

Electro pushes the Boom Ball.
It blasts loud music!

The team hears music.

"Let's check it out," Spidey says.

Electro hides from the heroes.

Team Spidey can't find
the Boom Ball.

Meanwhile, Electro takes
an Iron Man glove!

"Nothing can stop me!" says Electro.

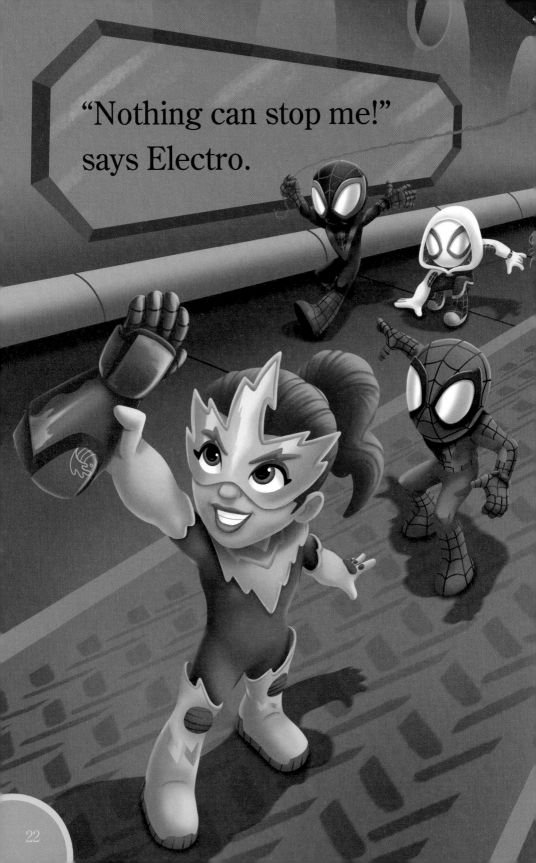

Electro tries the glove.
Water splashes her face!

Spidey thwips a glove
from Electro.

Iron Man contacts Spidey.
He says the call was fake.
"I'll be right back!"
Tony says.

Electro takes the
glove from Spidey!

The glove gives Electro
more power.

Miles sees the pool toy.
He has an idea.

The heroes put the pool
toy behind Electro.

Miles hurls a web ball
at Electro.

SPLASH!
Electro falls into the pool.
Her powers don't work!

Tony returns.
He thanks Team Spidey!

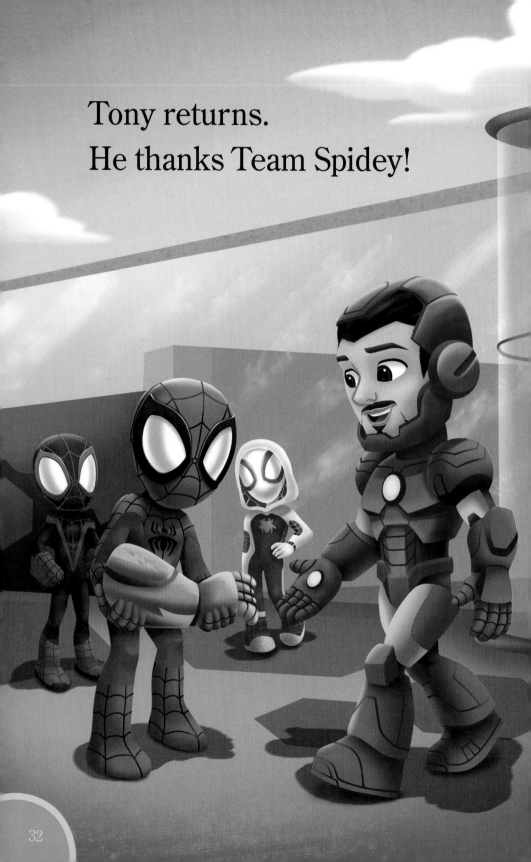